For Ailsa and Lyndall – B D

For Jammy and Esme – J P

LITTLE TIGER PRESS LTD,
an imprint of the Little Tiger Group
1 Coda Studios, 189 Munster Road, London SW6 6AW
www.littletiger.co.uk

First published in Great Britain 2020

Text by Becky Davies
Illustrations by Jennie Poh
Text and illustrations copyright © Little Tiger Press 2020

A CIP catalogue record for this book is available from
the British Library

Printed in China • LTP/1400/2983/1119

2 4 6 8 10 9 7 5 3 1

FSC
www.fsc.org
MIX
Paper from
responsible sources
FSC® C104723

The Forest Stewardship Council®(FSC®) is an international,
non-governmental organisation dedicated to promoting responsible
management of the world's forests. FSC operates a system of forest
certification and product labelling that allows consumers to identify
wood and wood-based products from well-managed forests.

For more information about the FSC, please visit their website at www.fsc.org

Little Turtle and the Sea

Becky Davies

Jennie Poh

LITTLE TIGER
LONDON

It began with a thunder storm.
   The rain lashed and the waves crashed as Little Turtle pushed her way out of the nest, and onto the sodden sand.

She needed to be quick. One flipper in
front of the other, she pulled herself down
the beach towards the sea, and safety.

Thunder rumbled in the sky as Little Turtle slipped into the sea for the very first time. The water rose to meet her and she was tossed and turned in the spray.

Which way was up? Tiny turtles splashed all around her, calling, "Swim, swim!"

Just when Little Turtle's flippers were tiring,
she managed to hitch a ride.

Her journey had begun!

Warm currents carried
Little Turtle over a carpet
of colour.

She danced with the swaying
seagrass. She swam with fish of
every shape and size.

"What beauty!" she said.
Happy and content, Little Turtle
climbed into a cosy cave and
slept.

Months passed, and Turtle
was no longer little.

She had outgrown her
hidey-hole . . .

. . . but she would never outgrow the ocean. Turtle swam onwards through mile after mile of dazzling open water.

She was quite alone, and yet she didn't
feel lonely. The ocean was her friend.

At last, Turtle's journey was complete. She had
made it to the other side of the world.

"Home," sighed Turtle.

And what a home it was!

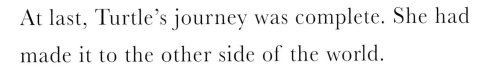

Foraging and feeding, Turtle lived there happily
for many years.

Until one day, it was time for her to return . . .

Turtle swam across the ocean, back to the beach where she had been born.

She made this journey many times, but found that the same journey was always different.

Turtle, too, was different. As she grew each year, her love for the ocean grew with her.

She saw new sights, made new friends and welcomed some new little turtles into the world.

Then one day, the ocean itself was different.

Colours disappeared, and Turtle found strange new creatures swimming beside her.

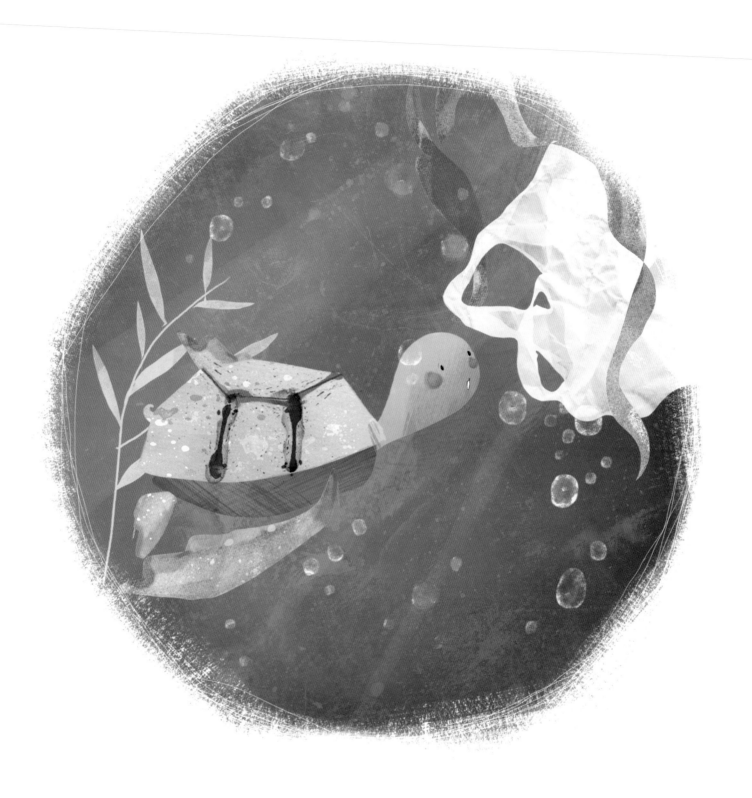

"Friend?" she asked. But she was met with silence.

The strangeness
grew and grew.

And Turtle felt lost in the
places she knew most.

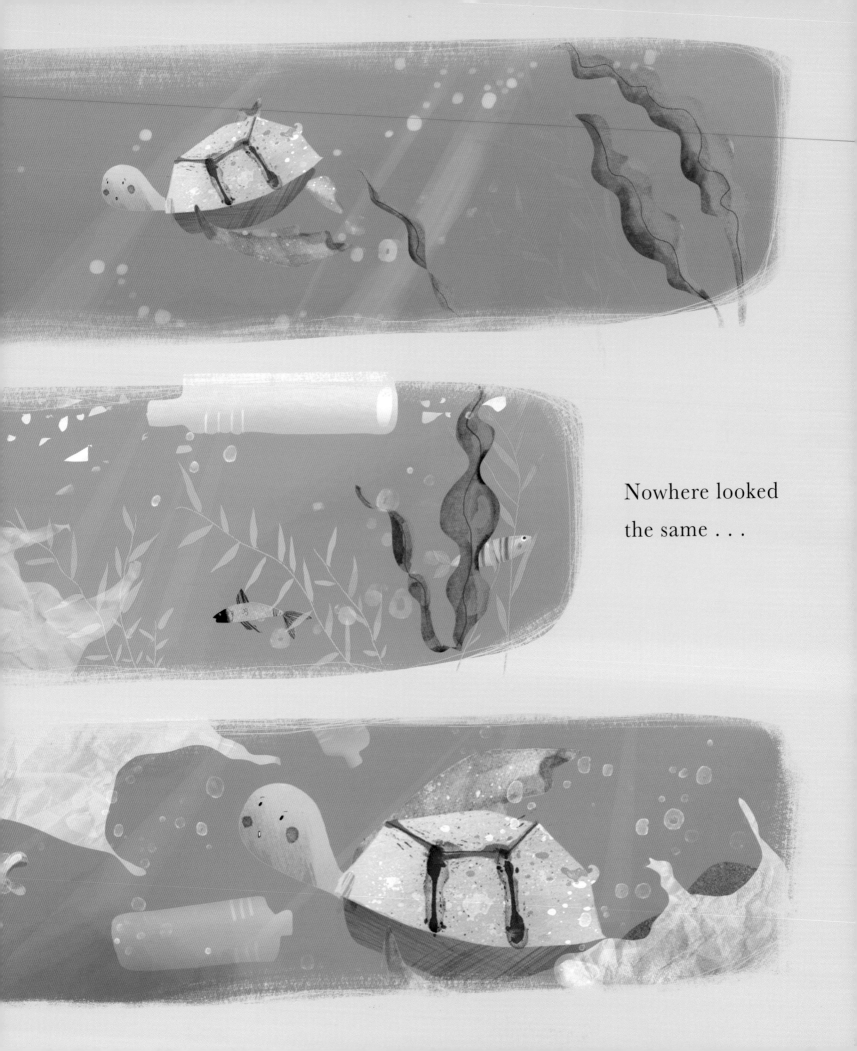

Nowhere looked
the same . . .

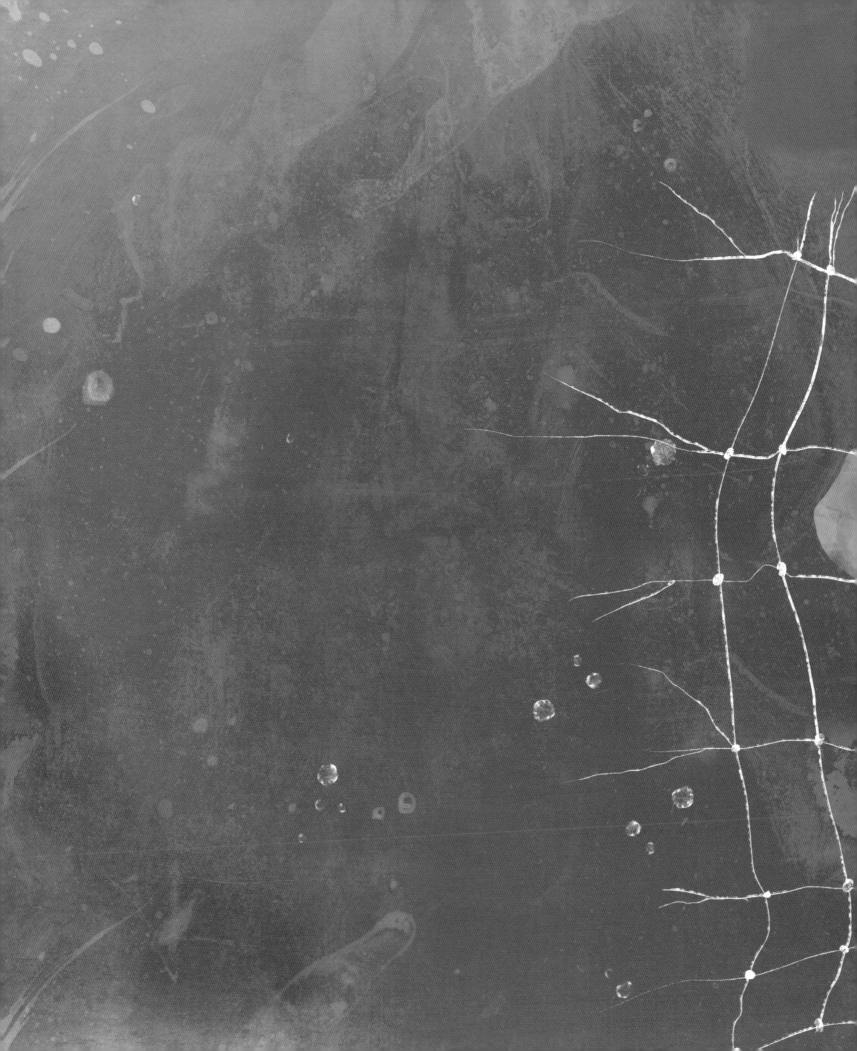

The ocean no longer felt like a friend.

"Hello?" she spoke into the darkness.

But Turtle was alone.

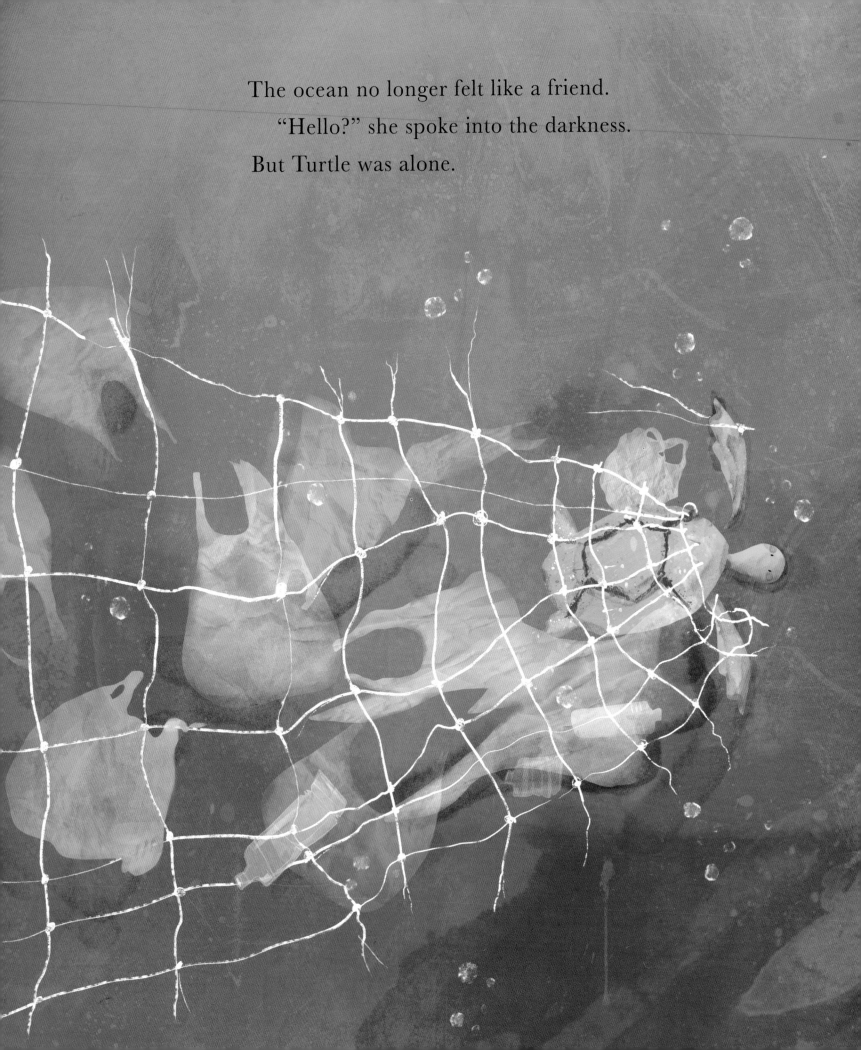

Just when Turtle thought
her journey was over forever,
figures emerged from the
strangeness and swam
towards her.

Turtle was freed!

Little by little, she watched as they tended the seagrass, the coral, and her friends.

"Thank you," she said. They had returned her to the ocean . . .

. . . and began to return Turtle's ocean to her.
It was beautiful once more, and she loved it
with her whole heart.

Note from the author

I've loved the ocean ever since I was little, when my family would take me on camping trips to Cornwall and we'd beach-hop our way around the county. It was a visit to Newquay in Cornwall that inspired me to write the story of Little Turtle, after I met a blind turtle called Omiros at an aquarium.

Omiros was rescued in Greece after being found tangled in fishing nets. His tank is big and lovely, but because of the damage to his eyes Omiros can never return home to the sea. All because of humans! Omiros is incredibly lucky, but I wonder if he knows what he's lost? Does he remember the ocean?

Our seas are steadily filling up with rubbish and plastic. Beautiful coral reefs are disappearing, and sea creatures all round the world are losing their homes. But it's not too late to do something about it – and all of us can help.

Glossary of terms

Biodegradable: When something is biodegradable, it means that when thrown away it breaks down into something already found in nature. If something is not biodegradable it will exist on Earth for a very long time!

Conserve: Protect something from being used up or harmed.

Coral: Corals are sea animals that stay in one place. Some types of coral build cases or skeletons, that stay in the sea after they die. After millions of years of growth, these cases form huge coral reefs which then provide homes to other sea creatures.

Landfill: A place where rubbish is buried in the ground.

Microplastic: Tiny pieces of plastic that don't break down. Sometimes they're so small that you can't even see them with your eyes, only under a microscope!

Pollution: Gases, smoke and chemicals that lead to unhealthy air, water or soil.

The Three Rs

Reduce: Cut down the amount we throw away.

Reuse: Give bags, bottles and other waste a second life by using them again, or . . .

Recycle: . . . make them into something new!

The plastic problem

When we throw plastic away instead of **recycling** it, it stays on Earth for a very long time. This is because plastic isn't usually **biodegradable**. If plastic gets put into **landfill** it can take up a lot of space, but it's worse if the plastic gets into our oceans – and it does!

How does our rubbish get into the ocean?

1. Down the drain. Drains lead to the ocean, so anything we flush like wet wipes, cotton balls and dental floss can end up in the sea.
2. Littering – and not just on the beach. Where does rubbish on the street go? Lots of it is collected, but it can be blown or washed into rivers and drains.
3. From the bin. Plastic from landfill sites is often blown away because it's so light.

The Great Garbage Patch

The Great Garbage Patch is a HUGE accumulation of rubbish in the Pacific Ocean. It's an area the size of the United States, Mexico and Central America put together! A lot of this rubbish comes from plastic like plastic bags, bottle caps, water bottles and Styrofoam cups. But some of it is so small you can barely see it, and this makes cleaning it up really hard! The rubbish is a swirling mess of **microplastics**, which are really dangerous to sea creatures. Groups like The Ocean Cleanup are doing everything they can to clear the ocean.

How plastic hurts marine life

They eat it – Loggerhead sea turtles often mistake plastic bags for their favourite food – jellyfish! Other sea creatures and birds confuse different plastics for food, and when they eat it their insides are damaged and they can die. **Microplastics** are so small that fish can eat them accidentally!

They get stuck in it – Seals, turtles and sea birds can get tangled in plastic fishing nets and bags, and they can't get free. Lots of sea animals have also become stuck in the plastic rings used to hold packs of drinks cans together.

How long does it last? Follow the timeline to find out.

Plastic straw
200 years

Plastic bag
10-20 years

Apple core and
cardboard box
2 months

What YOU can do to help!

Recycle as many cans, bottles and bags as you can.

Don't litter.

Drink tap water instead of bottled.

Only use a plastic bag if you really need one, and try to reuse it.

Reuse things you would usually throw away.

Don't use plastic straws, plates or cutlery.

Try to choose or buy things that don't have plastic wrapping.

Join a local litter pick event!

Plastic water bottle
450 years

Plastic drinks rings
400 years

Further reading

Mission: Sea Turtle Rescue: All About Sea Turtles and How to Save Them,
Karen Romano Young, National Geographic Children's Books, 2015

Somebody Swallowed Stanley, Sarah Roberts and Hannah Peck,
Scholastic, 2019

The Sea Book, Charlotte Milner, DK Children, 2019

What a Waste: Trash, Recycling, and Protecting our Planet,
Jess French, DK Children, 2019

Online resources:

https://www.natgeokids.com/uk/discover/animals/sea-life/
marine-wildlife-protection

http://www.kidsagainstplastic.co.uk

https://www.bbc.co.uk/newsround/39921749